T5-BBP-604

3 6277 15962282 0

BRESCIA COLLEGE
LONDON CANADA
FIDES ET VERITAS

ERRATA

GEORGE BOWERING

ERRATA

The Publishers
Red Deer College Press
56 Ave. & 32 St., Box 5005
Red Deer, Alberta, Canada T4N 5H5

Credits
Design & typesetting: Boldface Technologies Inc.
Cover art: Waldemar Kilinski
Printed in Canada by Hignell Printing Ltd.

Acknowledgements
The publishers gratefully acknowledge the financial contribution of the Alberta Foundation for the Literary Arts, Alberta Culture and Multiculturalism, and the Canada Council.

Canadian Cataloguing in Publication Data

Bowering, George, 1935-
Errata

ISBN 0-88995-040-7
I. Title.
PS8503.0875E7 1988 C818'.5408 C88-091526-9
PR9199.3.B63E7 1988

For Shirley Neuman, Smaro Kamboureli
and Linda Hutcheon

I may be wrong, but…

■ In the theatre, each member of the audience sees a different play because no two people are sitting in the same seat. This is much less true of the movies because the camera is in the middle, seeing for your eye. Those in the front of the movie theatre will feel a greater loyalty, perhaps, to a segment of the screen, but not much. Now, what about the readers of literature? A Montrealer reading *The Studhorse Man* probably sees it as a kind of more recent western; it happens (oh yes, mythically) out *there.* An intelligent reader in Leduc knows better than to look out the kitchen window for Demeter riding by; but her "out there" means outside the house. People who posit ideas such as The Canadian Tradition or The Northern Experience should travel less and spend time in more places.

■ People often ask, "What audience are you writing for?" But how can one write for an audience? One can read poems or stories to an audience. If one had the talent one could sing and dance for an audience, especially north of the fifty-fifth parallel. But when one is writing there is no audience there; at the best of times one is alone. Or nearly alone. There is no audience, but there is the text; one is alone except for the text. So one writes for the text. This is for you, one says, and one really hopes the text likes what one is doing. It is not, perhaps, the judge; but it is the significant and growing discernment one has to be aware of as company. When one happens to be the reader, producing the text that way too, one is also alone with the text. For instance, *Surfacing:* one is there, and the text is there—no one else.

■ Of course any text is an intertext. I had read other books and some forests before I read *Surfacing*. In reading fiction we can no more hope to avoid intertextuality than we can hope to avoid deconstruction. Once I thought of writing a use-anywhere critique called "Rifling the Canon: a study in continuous intertextuality." The continuousness of the attacks on unity is the only continuousness I can think of. Even a former reading of *Surfacing* will be woven into a new reading of the "same" novel. Some people, hearing such persnickity suggestions, will throw up their hands, the book flying from one of them, perhaps, and give up; they might say, "Oh, go and prattle elsewhere—leave me alone with my rereading, with my *plaisir!*" You are not rereading, I will say inside my head; pay attention—see? You are just reading.

■ The art in fiction, as in poetry, is that part of language that is not communication. In conversation (with my wife, for instance, she of the prodigious memory) I am often embarrassed by my failure to remember what happens in a novel I have read a year or two ago—*The Manticore,* for a recent example. Yet the half of me that likes to speculate in writer's theory says that such forgetting is not that important. Although recent novels by Robertson Davies may be described as page-turners, really it is the flavour of the mind we (not remember, but) remember tasting. How hopeless it is to try to convey that! Cole's Notes will never manage that experience, and neither will any film "version" of a novel. Communication works best when there is little sign of art. The Grecian Urn was more beautiful before John Keats got hold of it.

■ Here is the difference between the serious artist and, say, the politician, the businessman, or the social scientist: the more the serious artist gets to know about people, the less able he is to manipulate them. The realist writers always used to pretend that they were not manipulative; they used to say that their "characters" lived lives determined by environment and accumulative incidents, while the author only stayed around to observe. What a boon to their illusion were the clinics of Vienna and Zurich! But the best of them did not seize upon language as a tool to manipulate their readers, as Winston Churchill did with his evasive and hortatory abstractions or metaphors. Margaret Laurence, in *The Fire-Dwellers,* exhibits a great fondness for the words we have been gifted with, even while revealing the horror of their use by official terrorists.

■ If you will look at page 199 of the Bantam Books edition of Ross Macdonald's *The Chill* (1965), you will find this: "It was a well-worn copy of Yeats's *Collected Poems,* open to the poem, 'Among School Children.' The first four lines of the fourth stanza were underlined in pencil, and Bradshaw had written in the margin beside them the single word, 'Tish'." We published *Tish* from the fall of 1961 till the summer of 1963, when we were schoolchildren at UBC. Among our favourite predecessors in poetry was William Butler Yeats. Ross Macdonald went to a different Canadian university, one I was to attend after finishing at UBC. This is how intertextuality works best, as a series that looks accidental, that makes an order by apparent coincidence, synchronicity, let us say. But it is still unlikely that you will find a clue about *Tish* by reading those lines from Yeats. I dont remember checking.

■ My name is not Bower or Bowered. It is Bowering, so I suppose that the second word I ever learned to read looked like a present participle. Maybe I learned from the start of the written language to think of myself as an ongoing verb. Of course -ing is a patronymic of long standing. But at least two Canadian poets have written little poems in which they rimed my name with "flowering," and I appreciated that (especially given the possibilities). What I do is not write or written. It is writing. It is writing, and so am I. I am Bowering and I am writing. If you are reading, you are reading writing and Bowering, I hope. I am not a bower of bliss and I am not bowered with any muse; I am too busy bowering, I mean writing. You do see what I mean. It is writing and I am reading, and so are you. What is your name? Whatever it is, I hope you keep on doing it.

■ I dont want to read first-person narration in which the "I" is not writing. I see no point in the narrator's adopting the persona of a letter-writer, say, unless what I am reading is presented as writing done by that "I". If it's dictated to a scribe, okay. In the latter days of realism too many authors quit paying attention to writing as they attended to the world as referent. A similar thing happened in poetry when poets got so inattentive that they paid more attention to allusions than to vowels. I like *Famous Last Words* because I believe that I am reading silver words on resort walls. I know that both authors are writing as well as they can because of the problem of getting the words down and up. Some modernists retreated from plot and went inside the head, into a faked "stream of consciousness," for example. They never bothered to tell us how we readers got in there. They didnt seem to care about us readers.

■ Suppose that you are writing a novel. Let us call it a book. Let us suppose that like many writers, like Ethel Wilson in *Swamp Angel,* for example, you are trying to get the world right in your book, or, say, right into it. But really, if you should succeed in getting the world right in your book, you cant do it again that way, because now the world contains that book you have been writing. You would have to get the world, including now that book, right in that book. And you were probably not intending that at all. But at first the world did not contain that book and now it does. Your book, accepting both worlds, becomes discontinuous and plural, but is a world you are trying to get right like that? Maybe you can get the world right in your book for one sentence, and (but) then the world changes sentence by sentence because now your sentences are in it. I think that that is probably true, and it is exciting, a reason to go on in the world.

■ Early in our marriage, when we drove often over the face of North America, my wife would complain that I wanted to spend all my time on the highway rather than in the places along it. That was true. The highway *is* a place, I replied. But really it wasnt—driving was more like thinking. I felt real because travelling on the road resembled thinking; I was a Cartesian in a car. Thinking, too, has a constantly changing horizon which is always ahead and always behind, but mostly ahead, the past and the future, between which one is always moving, and *aware* of moving. Writing or reading a book, for instance *The Apprenticeship of Duddy Kravitz,* must be like that. But we do get the car home some time, and we get out of it for a while. Kravitz reaches denouement, and do you know what that means? Untying. Book as intricate knot rather than blacktop driving. And we usually take a plane when we go somewhere now.

■ When people talk about discontinuity, disjunction, disruption, and so forth, they are really remarking a break with habitual reading. Claude Simon has correctly pointed out that the real discontinuity was to be found in the long nineteenth-century realist texts, in which the narrator declared a distance from his own writerly concern, set the notion that the story he was telling was interchangeable with actuality, and then broke his characters' lives into little pieces with gaps between them. If the attention, as in *The Palace,* for instance, is given to the progress of the sentences rather than the events befalling the referent, there can be no question of discontinuity. Sentence follows sentence. There is no meanwhile, no later the same year, no in another quarter of the city. The next sentence is the next sentence to read, continuity, conjunction, narrative.

■ Dont get me "wrong"—I am not on a crusade against Realism. Realism was a brave adventure, and I was thrilled as I read the story of its course. There has never been anything wrong with Realism; only with what people thought it should try to do. What is important in the fictive event is not the possibility that it could happen in Chicago, but that the reader can imagine its happening in the book. That is what makes text. The reading, not the world, is the context. I read *The Pegnitz Junction* while I was living in Europe, but I had only the murkiest notion about where that train was. The story proposes destinations but nobody gets to them. However, we learn some fictive couple's real estate, even while the questions of residence and property are problematical in at least two "outside" worlds.

■ Writing on "The Dead," Richard Ellmann referred to modernism, as practised by T.S. Eliot and James Joyce, as "the imaginative absorption of stray material." When I read that phrase I took to it immediately. It posits by omission the notion of the individual creator, but it does not concern itself with him. In fact the grammar of the phrase leads right to the incoming. It lies just this side of Spicer's "writing from outside," and gives no validation to the personal unconscious at all, as far as I can see. Furthermore, it does not rank resources—so I would recommend it to my friends and relatives who accuse me of being a packrat of the trivial. Any stray material, once absorbed, becomes part of the solution. But there is something in post-modernist composition that welcomes the stray material and resists absorption. Charles Olson saw the poet himself as stray material, as an object among objects, not the solution, but one of the undissolved.

■ The difference between a long poem and a long novel is in the application of the word "long." A long poem is like a long play—it is the same length for all members of the audience, except for those who sleep or bolt the theatre. The so-called long novel is like a long corridor—some people will amble and others will dash its length. Rather, it is like a mansion of rooms—the tourist will decide not only how long to spend in it before going to the nearest cafe, but also how many rooms to visit and to some extent in what sequence to visit them. For this argument, *Wacousta* is an apt example. That is to say, or rather to repeat, a poem is a temporal event and a fiction is a spatial event. So the colloquial expression is more apt—a fat novel. In the event of a poem the time is determined and the space varies; in the event of a novel, the opposite is our experience.

■ If, in the making of your book, you indulge the language's whims rather than your own plan for dominance, some moron in the public press will call your work "self-indulgent." Probably some semi-amateur reviewer took on Robbe-Grillet's *Jealousy,* that amazing feat of making a first-person novel without a reference to the first person, and labelled it "self-indulgent." It appears that champions of authoritarian convention reach without analytical thought for authoritative clichés of the reviewer's trade. The enemies of "self-indulgent" writing favour standard practices, including things like description. In my opinion, that is where self comes to the fore, in the decision to present some referent in the author's power. There the author has to exhibit control over the other of language in order to dominate and represent the other of "landscape," his term for places and people.

■ I am just working away contentedly in my avant garden. We always have to put up with the social responsibility of the terms—how they would sneer when they assigned you to the "avant-garde," or the "experimental." Now we have to decide whether to blush when they say "post-modern" and so on. "Post-everything," they say. I have known the name of Gertrude Stein all my life, and have read her seriously for twenty years. I guess that when all is said and done I will settle for what they gave her: I will be someone who did not write books like *Fifth Business,* to be placed in the mainstream of Canadian literature, but all the same someone whom they cannot write a history without mentioning. He was always pottering around in his garden, they will say, and once in a long while someone would come around and, well not really admire, but perhaps enquire about the odd-looking shrubs.

■ When I was young and intending to be a writer, and writing stories and probably poems, I continued the contrariness I had always practised as a kid. It seemed the logical way to escape common thought, which must be not good enough, and it was an instinct. So I instinctively distrusted the satisfaction of understanding. Now I know how to practise and describe a *methodos*, so I say that I function by and through misunderstanding. Maybe I should say dis-understanding. I know that my favourite books have always been the ones I could not really understand but which I could see immediately and could immediately see would last all through my life. An example would be *The Unnameable*. I really understand detective books, so now I cannot remember them. I feel a similar way about writing. I dont even mind if my readers think they understand, as long as they do not really understand the most important stuff.

■ What does one want one's readers to learn and know? Is it the world, pictured and referred to? Is it the details of one's childhood and defloration and problematical present life? No, they already know all that, or they can easily find it elsewhere, in or out of books. Here is what one wants his reader to learn and know: that writing and imagining can be done, can still be done. One wants them to notice thinking, not to buy thought. That's thinking, not thinking about. If I remember anything about my favourite books, such as *Tristram Shandy,* it is not what objects had things happen to them, or what people did what. I can usually remember next to nothing about what people mistakenly say is the action of the novel. But I always remember what was actually happening—language tracks that told me there was a really interesting kind of thinking going on. Those tracks are still here.

■ I guess I write to trick reality into revealing itself. I dont think that I can do that by using realism. Realism is a belief as well as a practice, and reality is aware by now of how it approaches, and thus where to go and hide. You have to treat reality like a cat. Chances are that a dog will come, like confessional description, when you call it; but to entice a cat you have to appeal to its curiosity, or make it think that it is making the approach. Artists and writers, and even philosophers have been after reality for centuries. Sometimes they find it and get a good look. They got a good look and told about it in *Sister Carrie*. But reality has learned that approach, so no writer will ever be able to use Dreiser's method again. If you use Dreiser's method now you will end up with novels such as those written by Arthur Hailey.

■ I have recently read that 200 million years ago a considerable land mass completed a voyage from the South Pacific, to fetch up against us and become Vancouver and Quadra Islands. Yet some people less than a century old are still criticizing me for not knowing deeply the human writing (for instance, *The Heart of the Ancient Wood*) that makes up their version of the Canadian tradition. I tell them my biographical and geographical reasons for my ignorance of their regional literature, but their response is that I should strive to overcome the accidents of my birth and rearing. I recognize their attitude. I used to hear it (and still do hear it from immigrant academics) from purveyors of British folkways in my various B.C. homes. But tradition, in the post-Victorian age, is not even determined anymore. We now choose our traditions. The International Modernists, who were neither British nor Canadian, showed us that. I do not give up my birthright when I choose Ruben Darío over Charles G. D. Roberts or Kingsley Amis.

■ I have always been impatient with the easy use of the term "experimental" as it is attached by reviewers and others to unorthodox writing. When Zola used the term in his famous essay, he was firm in his analogy with laboratory science, and his emphasis was upon the experimenter's detachment. An experiment proceeds from a theoretical position, and results most often in a mental product to be discarded or amended. Experimental writing, most often, should not be published, though a report on the experiment might be. I am often an experimenter. During some years, for example, I planned to try a story based on the fact that the Italian word *stanza* means room. In the story a traveller would be shown into a room, and would confront all the material in a stanza of a famous poem. Then I elected to try one of Ezra Pound's cantos instead of a stanza. I experimented with every canto, and found out that this experiment, like most, clarified the question by failing.

■ A story goes that some years ago a would-be writer persisted so long in importuning Margaret Atwood to write a recommendation for her Canada Council grant application that Atwood eventually filled in the blanks this way: I have known the applicant _0_ years, in my capacity as complete stranger. Quite often I hear from unknown poets, sculptors, etc., who take it for granted that I should give them my total support because we are both, after all, artists. But for years I have learned to live in the middle of a seeming contradiction. Socially and politically I believe that I am a romantic leftist; but when it comes to the composition of literature I am an elitist. I am not reluctant to say that I'm interested in the art of writing. I like trade unions and hate chambers of commerce, but I am still not going to support an unlearned instinct poet in her delusion that she deserves the attention I will give happily to *The Dumbfounding.*

■ There are many readers who are made anxious by writing that is open. They somehow feel more secure if the poem has consistent rime and meter, or if the story closes all the doors and turns out the lights, and then a good night's sleep. Closure seems to mean to them a "good read." They can close *Each Man's Son* like a door. Maybe they are closed outside the book, but so is the book safely locked out of the room, its words only facing one another on the pages. But I dont think that I am protected by closure. I think that closure protects the writing from me, the reader. I cant squeeze in front of that terminal juncture; I cant make any decision regarding multiplicity; I cant reply to the monolog. It is not that I want to hurt that closed-up writing. It is not that I want to force my point of view. I just want to know it's not over, not

■ Some of them say that any text is defiled as soon as it is written down; that is a credo for some people. Others say that all variations on the text are fine, that they are the fuel with which the reader activates her work, the ignition of the poem. I am drawn with all my conscious heart to both positions. They are perhaps mutually contradictious. That is how it is to be a writer/critic these days. The avant-garde has shifted: once the writers were the avant-garde; now the critics are. They please you very much with their wicked, lovely phrases. The Derrida ones, the Lacan ones, the Shklovsky ones, the Bahktin ones. Maybe even the Benjamin ones. They please you. And you want to please them. If you say that a text is defiled before they get it, you are a romantic idealist. If you say that they have to generate the poem, given a version of your text, you are a progressive egalitarian. I, for one, always wanted to be those two.

■ I dont know what will happen to fiction writing now that parents can buy contoured throw-away diapers for their brats. Diapers used to be white cloths cut in the shape of a page. We had our pattern set for us and pinned together tight. Every time we did some writing our anthologists or critics said it was time for a change. They always paid close attention to our latest works. They praised us when we produced something solid for the first time. They got worried if we became fixated on the text, if we started playing with it. They knew that structure was important, but they directed us to subject. Did we see the contemporary environment as a waste land or a new world? Reflexivity was not in their plans; they were after growth. They promoted referentiality. They looked forward to our dispensing with the page, to the time when we would sit and think, and be regular writers.

■ "Memory," wrote Roland Barthes, "is the beginning of writing, and writing is in its turn the beginning of death (however young one is when one undertakes it)." Barthes said that in a particular context, in his great essay on Chateaubriand, but I believe that it applies wherever you will look, even to the antehistorical beginning of all writing (which, I believe, follows reading and precedes speech). My first unpublished novel, the 550-page *Delsing,* grew (and foundered) on my perfect recall of all sensations to the time at which I wrote it, in my early twenties. I then forgot nearly everything up to that time—my childhood and adolescence were dead. As soon as one looks at life, reads it, and then writes *about* it, it is a corpse. That is a great story. The novelist, then, lives the rest of his deaths, and may dedicate himself to the life of our language.

■ I like photographs rather than paintings or drawings, rather than art, to decorate my books. On the cover or inside, I prefer photographs. Photographs happen now, and then, now and then. But art always happens when. No matter how active, art comes from somewhere like eternity and is pointing its nose, and ours, toward eternity. The photograph is "taken" or made in perhaps one five-hundredth of a second. Think what a second is to eternity, and then think of five hundred possible photographs in that time. My books are that far away from the perfect. But look how much light there was available in one five-hundredth of a second! It is not that a photograph is more real than a drawing—it is only that you know it was made more by light than by you. I keep hoping that that is true about my books—or something that feels like that. Writing can be so nice when it is a snap.

■ An historical-geographical novel I wrote in the Seventies was called *A Short Sad Book.* I tried to cover the nation, with scenes set in every province. One day on Burnaby Mountain a famous stage actress from Saskatchewan told me she had read the novel and that I had perfectly captured the scene of a lonely Saskatchewan railroad station on a bitterly cold day in deep winter. She said that she could remember it perfectly and asked me when I had been there. But I have never been at a Saskatchewan railroad station on a cold winter's day. I told her I had made it all up out of words, including the part about how the cold wind blowing against the skirt of a woman felt on the fronts of her thighs. Well, said the actress, it was exactly the way she remembered it. It was really real, she said. That was the only chapter in which I had attempted description rather than my usual procedure. It just goes to show how easy description is when you've got a prairie.

■ Italo Calvino, in his marvelous essay on the combinative process, said that the author is in charge of a machine without knowing how it works. That is perhaps how I drive a car. The author is looking a little way down the road his sentences are becoming, and gliding with a kind of hip *gnosis.* Not to get somewhere, let us say, but to be getting there. Scholars make much of Joyce's multi-tiered allusive structures, but surely the joy in reading Joyce is in sharing his pell-mell plunge down the sentence and knowing that neither of you understands how the thing keeps going. There is gravity, and finally the book falls into the bookseller's hands or onto the critic's desk. One knows that a writer like Robertson Davies, for all his scholarly spooks, does not want to drive over the speed limit. But while one is reading *Beautiful Losers* one is aware that Leonard Cohen does not know what in hell he is doing so damned well.

■ Once I was looking at a man sitting at a coffee counter in the Ottawa airport. A flight number was called over the public address; he pulled out his ticket and checked it. Later a name was called over the p.a.; he pulled out his ticket and checked it again. Here was a man bedevilled by uncertainty, and not put to any comfort by authority, an authority he wanted to consult. He could have been a conventional reader forced to play a role in a postmodern fiction. If *Gone Indian* had begun in central Ottawa's airport instead of marginal Edmonton's airport that man would have been a marginalized central character, at least for a small scene. What does he mean? In my notebook I have been wondering for ten years, while the Ottawa airport has been displaced by the new Ottawa airport. Robert Kroetsch said, "The minute you ask answerable questions, you're beat as a novelist." There's hope in that.

■ There is a certain western literary critic, take Warren Tallman, for instance, who was born into the new frontier, and writes essays for readers who have to grow up in neutron fear. What a strange and problematic position to be in! Warren Tallman, for instance, grew up around gas stations in the Pacific Northwest, where modernism was likely eventually to reach, where regret lived out the decline of Joseph Conrad as the news in trans-oceanic writing, where Henry James was cherished because so remote. Well, then, modernism, but dont give it a name. Warren Tallman, for instance, did not really know what they were saying about literary composition in the Ivy League, so he just listened to whatever he could hear, and luckily that was language. Now there is a reaching even here in our Pacific Southwest of postmodernism, in which the critics are the famous writers; but Warren Tallman, for instance, is stuck with writing, back there, when the language is new.

■ When I was a kid, and was trying to know what people who knew know, I was always told about writing that the best was that that was very clear and seemed effortless. I was let in on the secret that it took a lot of effort to make the writing appear effortless, and that that was good, that the writer should be congratulated if he could pull it off. So I believed it. But for some reason I didnt practise it in fiction, though I certainly did in poetry. In fiction I kept giving in to those things that were fun, and of course I felt guilty about roiling the surface that was supposed to be limpid. That was their favourite word: limpid. I always suspected that word somehow. People who said it always seemed so highly pleased with themselves. So I wrote prose that was not like *The Heart of the Matter.* I confess it: I like to make the craft visible and the referent invisible.

■ A small number of us on the West Coast make much of what we call dictated poetry. It is something we cherish as against the exploitive will, against the order of subjective description and anecdote. Of course we recite the examples Rilke, Yeats and Spicer. But of course we are not mesmeroids; we are more likely to be scholastics of verse practice. In an essay called "Concerning 'Adonis'," Paul Valéry probably most honestly or accurately put our case: "The gods in their graciousness give us an occasional first line *for nothing*; but it is for us to fashion the second, which must chime with the first and not be unworthy of its supernatural elder." In this way, failing or not, we turn our ears to the poem—it is its turn to take our attention. We will insult that first line the second we turn our hungry regard upon some "subject." We are priests, not monarchs. We have no subjects. A gift from the gods is not a licence to rule.

■ I never wanted to write an autobiography. I think that certain works I have done with what looks like my life story should be called biotext. The problem with the historians, or let us say the way they chose to work, is this: they did not study what people are, but what they did. They were more interested in time than in place. So literary historians did not much address what books are, but rather who wrote them and how they fit into the time of their societies. Hence the deprivileging of literary form—the very place where the writer of the poem or the fiction found himself. Michael Ondaatje, in "Rock Bottom," created biotext, or it got created for him. Readers of *Running in the Family* know right away that they are not getting history, not getting autobiography. Autobiography replaces the writer. Biotext is an extension of him.

■ There are two different reactions by peoples who have come to find themselves rejecting their images as historical victims. In the east the easterners try to get their own history. In the west we westerners try to get something else. In Montreal they want their young to read and live the new history of Quebec. In Toronto they want the history of Canada instead of the appendix to the history of Britain or Babylon. In the west we make *Tay John*, the West Edmonton Mall, and bill bissett. We think we live west of history, so when we write historical novels, their heroes are born out of ground rather than time. We tried history, and it beat us; that's why we came here. If you want to enter the west you have to check your history at the door. Easterners, also known as realists, tell us that if we dont stay in their history the Americans will get us. But just as the Romans learned their subjects' languages the better to rule them, so the Americans will try to learn your history. Better not have any.

■ The best poetry is written in fear. I dont know about the best fiction; maybe the best fiction is the best poetry. But the best poetry is written in fear. When it has a good reader, the best poetry is read in fear. When I was a child I did not believe that a dog could have eyes as large as mill stones, but when I heard the words telling about it, I was scared smaller than I was. And by something mainly prose. All that subjectivist descriptive poetry filling the Ontario poetry papers and quarterlies could not scare anyone, certainly not the poettes. Great poetry does not tell you things about some poet's day or family. But *Duino Elegies* and *The Triumph of Life* gather up as much skill as the human soul can muster and leave safe soil behind, to lay human song at the doorsill of the gods' music room. There, there is no courage, no time for courage, no space. Only the fear. Only the beloved icy torrent of fear.

■ In *The Treatise of Human Nature,* David Hume, my longtime hero, said: "Carelessness and in-attention alone can afford us any remedy. For this reason I rely entirely upon them." Two centuries later, Charles Olson remarked that he treated misprints in his poems as departures for the part of the imagination that wants to hear where words will lead. The continuity of the damned human will is the writer's (and especially the reader's) main enemy. Most of what we might discover is bypassed when we treat human sentences as message-bearers, dispensible when they reach their target. The quick brown fox jumps over the lazy dog, but the dog can follow any scent that diverts him, in patterns that are never there till he is. Follow David Hume's scent far enough and you'll get to Heidegger. Follow Heidegger and you'll forget there ever was a topic sentence. Mona Hodgson, my grade eleven English teacher, ran weeping from the room. Guess what she wrote on my report card.

■ I suppose that "setting" in a fiction is not truly equivalent to a set on a stage, a stage set for a play. But many of us can be persuaded that some such equivalency will serve. Thus the author of *Two Solitudes* will spend a leisurely page setting the stage, or let us say describing the location before he puts his characters into it. But there is another, basically phenomenological, view that would not be able to conceive or perceive a horizon even theoretically independent of the human, character or narrator. This view does not like perspective much. The place, the "out there," is not prior to human perception or activity; it is a result of someone's being in the world. "Environment" is not possible, because one cannot be surrounded by something he is part of. The writer's words call the fictional place into being. The human being's presence is the first language.

■ It is one thing to say that we can learn by paying attention to nature. It is another thing to regard nature as a teacher. Nature is not a teacher. Not a teacher, not a mother, not a lover, not an enemy, not a friend, not a rival. Nature does not brood or exult or bend a loving face. The Romantics used to speak of love and terror in nature, but they spent their time in England or Italy. Anywhere you go in England or Italy, you can dig straight down in the earth and find old culture. Or read *Towards the Last Spike*: the poet would seem to be writing about the crossing of nature, but he does it in really artificial language. Breathing is natural, but it does not teach anyone how to write poetry. Poetry teaches poetry. Art teaches art. But nature does not even teach nature. Nature cannot learn. Poets can learn but nature cannot teach. It can only be what is learned. A poet must learn that nature cant teach him anything.

■ For years I was a poet who liked to read novels; and I thought that would be quite the usual thing. But I kept hearing from other poets, older and younger, that they did not read novels. They read poetry, and such things as *The Origin of Consciousness in the Breakdown of the Bicameral Mind.* I kept hearing that, really, poets do not have time to read novels. I decided to find out whether I could be an aberration: I would keep on reading novels because I love them so much, and I would try to be a poet, nevertheless. I have never found out how novels hurt a poet. Was it because novels are just made up, and the poet needs all his reading time to find material in the scientific world; or was it because novels are the repository of second-rate imaginative writing? In any case, I got the message that no part of one's reading of a novel will do one any good in the writing of poetry. That's probably true.

■ I have often explained that I wrote the first third of *Burning Water* in Trieste in order to elude the temptation to describe the British Columbia coast. Read on. At the waterfront in Trieste you could see perhaps two centimeters into the green black water where the little *Christine* and the little *Capo Matapan* lie rolling as the Adriatic mist burns off. Expert teenage lovers look moony and kiss their girls. An hour ago and six blocks away you were in the Alps. Now you are in the Mediterranean, where Slavs speak fast Italian and it is "good for you" to sit in the November sun. You are sitting now in the only park you know where cats and pigeons lie in the sun together. A couple of human beings walk by in mauve jeans and twin "Houston A's" jackets. There are no Houston A's. "In June 1916, while Marie Taxis watched through a spyglass from her hotel balcony in Trieste as Duino was being destroyed by Italian grenades, Lord Kitchener went down with the cruiser *HMS Hampshire* off the Orkneys in the North Sea."

■ There is something interesting about literary history as opposed to normal history. Literary history is about books, and if you want to you can read those books. You can read *The History of Emily Montague* if you really want to. But you could never read Emily Montague, even if history said there was an Emily Montague. You can go to the Plains of Abraham, but you will not see the battle. Montcalm is dead. But you can read a famous old novel, and then you can read about it in literary history. Montcalm may be found only in history, but you have to go away from literary history to find a novel. What induces your love of a novel is its form; but literary history deprivileges form. Historians do not study what books are but what they did, and how they fitted their society. Historians are interested in time, but novels take place. Novels are here, but history is now and then.

■ In her *New Yorker* profile of March 1978, Jeanne Moreau was quoted as saying: "The deeper you go into life, the more you have to forget." Since that time I have been waiting for that to seem to have something to do with what I find myself saying. I wonder now, though, whether that is "have to" or "have." Also, I wonder whether "deeper" means later. Well, I do not care whether Moreau is talking about moral matters. I am interested in forgetting. When I was a college student I wrote a long novel about everything that had happened to me till I was twenty-one. I could remember everything, including how late afternoon South Okanagan October sun glinted off the purple-blue roof of a 1948 Mercury sedan. I tried to do unusual writing, but it came out as realism. Memory condemns one to sentimentality, which means attachment to things, and to realism, famous for its detachment. Later I learned to give up memory. Keep your mouth shut, memory. Memory can do you no good if you want to make books instead of just writing them down.

■ I have been, on a few occasions, in those beer parlours in which young women move around on a little stage, taking all those erotic clothes off to the sound of some teenage music from a cassette tape player. When their third song is finished they gather their cast-off raiment and make their way off the stage to some small place behind a wall. Sometimes one may see them later in the room, in their ordinary street clothes. It is then, invariably, that they look most interesting, even sexiest. Even though the woman on the stage is pretending some stock erotic drama, using symbolic attire, her nakedness is finally bare fact, the given. The stuff of realism. Later, in tight jeans or a jumpsuit, she is not the given but the disguised, or the artificed. The stuff of composition. People say, "I *love* your blouse." They dont say, "I *love* your pubis." So you see that naked realism is always pretending, while fictive composition is always more inviting of the curiosity.

■ Lionel Kearns and I used to have public debates, in front of classes, on cable television, on panels, in which I took the elitist position regarding the making of poetry, and he stated the populist view. His position, simplified, was that any person can be a poet and write poetry. I said that poets were something like priests, who had to meet a vocation with intense training. I think that *Death of a Lady's Man* is a completely different order of event from the things that happen in *Quarry* magazine. Let me put it this way: as in the beaver we may see the potential of the engineer, so in the ordinary literate human being we may see the potential of the poet. We know that the beaver can stop a lot of water, but he will never build an observatory. I dont know how many busy beavers there are in Canada, but the League of Canadian Poets says that there are hundreds and hundreds of poets here. I have to say that I am glad that the beavers cannot write English or French.

■ There is something about telling stories in books that makes you be more careful than in telling stories out loud. You know that people can check and analyze. Girls have books thrust on them, and when they become women they write stories in books. I feel that writing stories in books is female, and suggests realism. Oral tale-telling is male, and suggests braggadocio or bullshit. I know that women are supposed to like to talk, and men suffer in silence. That is another matter. But when women tell stories out loud, they report what happened and what people said. When men write stories in books they can hardly wait to stop the story. So what happens in *Badlands*? The author had to write the story as a woman, to get it down, because none of the men in the story would get it done. When she throws her father's "end of words" into the lake she walks away, and she says that she "did not once look back, not once, ever." But of course the whole book, written after that walk, is made of looking back. The author had to be a woman to do that.

■ If it is correct to speak of a writer as an artist, I am an escape artist. As a novelist and as a poet, I take as my master Harry Houdini. Or put it in criminal terms, as certain French writers like to do. I think of my text as a getaway car. Let them sift through the evidence at the scene of the crime, or let them pursue me along the highway. I intend, by the time they have their wits together, to be in the next province. Yet I do want to leave clues—that is why I write in normal English sentences, and why I leave my fingerprints all over everything. In these days people call that "signature." I would really like to leave behind me, among them, the kind of text I have cherished most: the kind that you read in your youth and know you do not understand, but which you know you will read all your life, hoping to understand more of in your maturity.

■ Margaret Laurence loved attaching other people's words to her books. She attached children's songs, passages from the Bible, bits of poetry by Dylan Thomas, Carl Sandburg and Al Purdy, found poetry printed on African trucks. Attached to the beginning of *This Side Jordan* is this proverb from West Africa's Akan people: "Oh God, there is something above, let it reach me." Our critics have certainly been right in insisting on Laurence's connection to our earth; even the writers who keep calling her "the mother of us all" (though Margaret Laurence does not resemble Gertrude Stein) intend that "mother" to call up Mother Earth. But Laurence and her expressionistic protagonists are always looking to heaven, for assurance, for an argument, for a *connection.* Stacey MacAindra would be upset to learn for sure that the God she doubts is not there to hear her complaints. In that she is what Margaret Laurence really is, a daughter as we all are.

■ Mother Earth or mother tongue. It is from our mothers that we learn the grammar of our speech and of the speech we put into the mouths of the people we turn into characters. In *The Mother of Us All* Gertrude Stein has her central figure, Susan B. Anthony, say: "We cannot retrace our steps, going forward may be the same as going backwards." Especially if our steps are stepping into a river, especially if, as Morag Gunn told us, "The river flowed both ways." Earth, river, fire to dwell in—no wonder Margaret Laurence looked for something above, to let it reach her. Looked up as daughters do to their mothers, to learn a grammar for living. In this regard, Margaret Laurence, Peggy Wemyss, was the sister of us all. She did not teach us to speak—she taught us that we had to learn to speak. She wrote the novel that our teachers would call our best ever, and then she went out and tried to learn how to write a novel.

■ In "An Essay on Virginia," William Carlos Williams, the father I chose, said: "Unity is the shallowest, the cheapest deception of all composition. In nothing is the banality of the intelligence more clearly manifested." Consistency is the hobgoblin of something or other. Here is the anti-teleological anarchism the nationalists and other totalitarians hate. But you see how unity is made in an item of literature: a will has to insist on a center outside of which must remain the unbidden. A product of such activity can be beautiful. A uniformed army of blond men all two meters tall is perhaps beautiful. Sorry, that is probably unfair argument. All right: why do people call for unity? Because they desire strength, or think they do. Should we really enter the act of composition looking for strength? I dont think so. I want to make a book you can get your fingers into, to break it open.

■ One doubts the value of socialist state art when one sees that fascist regimes call for a similar style. Recently we saw the embarrassment in Hungary when a poster was seen to be plagiarized from a Nazi poster fifty years old. I do not mean simply a doubt of the value to art and its world; I mean also a doubt of the value of the prescribed art to society. Obvious symbolism, for example—overly muscular workers, flags carried into the wind—promotes the arrival of cynicism with the advent of maturity, an unfortunate coincidence. I believe that art, including literature, does have a social responsibility. But it does not owe its forms to the state. A state (or a business elite) that will dictate the lineaments of human beings depicted in sculpture or fiction will try to dictate the thoughts of human beings outside the text. When one statue can replace another without changing the surround in respect to it, one sees an attitude to art that would be called racism if it were an attitude toward human beings.

■ We designate the literary eras of earlier centuries by giving them names according to reigns: Elizabethan drama, neo-Augustan poetry, Victorian prose. In our own century we replace reigns with wars, or rather the times between wars: pre-WW II fiction, post-Vietnam verse. We are probably saying that in our century, since the advent of aerial bombardment and International Modernism, inherited literary tradition has gone the way of inherited rule. Whereas a poet such as Wordsworth, for all his Napoleon and all his speech of common men, would consider himself a continuation of the English tradition that made Milton, the twentieth-century writer lives in a world that expects revolution with every generation. The wars we have seen change the world forever, and our writers do not expect to elaborate on the work of their dead predecessors—they expect to rewrite them. We do not write Elizabethan II literature. We all write postwar writing.

■ When we quote from the writing of, say, Jacques Derrida, we do not do so in order to be polite to Derrida, nor to give him credit for the development of our thought and argument; we do it because we wish it to be known that we too have read Derrida. If it is possible, we make endnotes for those prospective readers who scan the page of references for their own names. When we get a little more sophisticated in this game, we look for less common names to mention, preferably for hyphenated names that look European, especially Eastern European, at least uncommon, with "X's" in them, perhaps. Perhaps the names of people mentioned by Derrida's students. In doing all this, we probably become educated, in a way. We make our stodgy colleagues afraid of us or scornful of us, responses that are equally welcome. They will tend to leave us alone in our offices, where we can then find the time to re-read Jean-Louis Houdebine.

■ In a book entitled *As We Know,* John Ashbery said this about our contemporary writing: "We must first trick the idea/Into being, then dismantle it." Compare that process with the one described by Paul Valéry: "The gods in their graciousness give us an occasional first line *for nothing*; but it is for us to fashion the second, which must chime with the first and not be unworthy of its supernatural elder." John Ashbery's name chimes with Paul Valéry's, but his words tell us of our difficulty in faith now that we are in the postmodern condition. We no longer read the metanarrative of the gods, nor even of the modernist substitution, the authority of art. The new poet is a trickster without a Creator, a Coyote without an Old Man, to use western Amerindian names. The idea he tricks into being is not the art. The dismantled fragments, shapes shifted to bits, are not his art. The dismantling is his art, a de-processing that cannot be kept in a museum with any imaginary Grecian urns.

■ Often, I think, the serious writer must ask himself whether writing is a useful way to spend his time. I know that I come to the conclusion (which never lasts) that writing is useless. Then why, you ask, do you go on writing? You might add some phrase such as "you silly nit." Why spend so much effort at it? Something similar might be asked of you, reader (though I will not append an *ad hominum* insult). Why do you spend so many of your unreplenishable hours in reading things such as novels and poems? Or something such as this—you can, if you so desire, stop right now, or let us say right here. Currently, or I should say that at the time of the writing of this, I am half-way through *Not Wanted on the Voyage*. You could put my book down right now. The pages ahead of you dont matter. Timothy Findley's sweater. But why bother. If you have a good reason not to stop reading, to get eventually to such a phrase as "the walk along Inglis Street is metonymic," that is understandable. But the fluid . . . .

■ I want a clean, well-lighted place. She wants a room of one's own. I am a writer and she is a writer, too. I want a room of my own with good lighting. He is a writer, and so am I. Even if it is not clean, it must be well-lighted. I want to write there, to be where there are a few others in the night. If she writes in Jacob's room is it one's own? He is never there any more. If it is your own room, you are responsible for keeping it clean. Well, is that what a man wants, a place that is so well-lit that it has to be kept clean? He is afraid of the dark and dirt. Why not? She cant take it any more, living in those rooms other people are free not to write in. Women who are to be writers need rooms of their own, and not just to keep clean. As long as the prose is clean, so we men can live in it and say it was sure worth it, he getting that room at last.

■ The writing that results from what some of my favourite writers might do could be the result of, let's say, a brain derailment. No more choo choo. But lots of debris. North America became a continent in our minds when all the last spikes were driven; Canada became Canada at Craigellachie; or rather in Ottawa and Toronto, where men in suits looked at a photograph taken at Craigellachie. The faces in the photograph launched a thousand locomotives and poems. Our sentences could be continuous from sea to sea. On the railway, time and regularity are cherished, even if seldom tidy. Our critics and teachers and anthologists looked for a smooth-running literature, to ensure the survival of the Canadian fact. Now, thank goodness, the untamed redskins are out there sabotaging the tracks. The *Martyrology* is a shipment that will never get here from headquarters. A brain derailment has scattered it all over the landscape off the right-of-way; and we scavengers have our aprons filled.

■ All reading of fiction is deconstruction, but film-watching is not, because the speed at which we watch it is not a producer of meaning; it is not difference. In sitting and watching a film, the watcher is not a reader; there can be no voluntary deferral in the act, or rather the passive reception. In other words one would have to operate the machinery to be involved in text production. Video helps. In fiction, narrative is produced by the turning of the page, which is an option every time. In movies you can have deconstruction only by reference—deconstruction of the world, or deconstruction of the medium. The Road movies of Bing Crosby and Bob Hope were made by disruption—references to the previous movie, or asides to the cinema patrons. But that disruption, or its recognition, is coerced. On the other hand, in reading a novel, a reader deconstructs it from word to word, dispersing it through his psychic space.

■ Paranoid people report that their bodies, or sometimes just their heads, have been taken over, used by someone else, some alien, some oppressor, perhaps. They dont like it. It frightens them. They hear voices telling them things they dont want to hear. We poets, when we want to impress laymen with the extraordinary procedure of poetic composition, claim similar things without complaint; or if we do complain, of the torture of such poetic seizure, for instance, we do so to promote the image of our sacrificial sensitivity. Even if we dont believe that paranoics are bedevilled by remote mind-controllers, we think there is something wrong with their stories and behaviour. We doubt them. We doubt the poets, too, but by convention we respect their sensitivity. Are poets just paranoics who write their messages down? We are certainly more comfortable with frenzy that results in order. By their ordering the poets show their value to our version of the world.

■ I have always favoured tapinosis. I like to commit it and I like to be an audience for it. Tapinosis is a sneaky kind of rhetoric—it means the saying of very serious things in offhand language, in vernacular, even in slang. When I lecture, I even like to lecture *en tapinois.* Somehow, I believe that the steganographic sentiment is the more deeply felt and more seriously received—if it is not missed entirely. Probably there is an element of puritanism in my reverse-occultism. I remember that in American war movies the G.I.s were always saying they had just gone through hell, whereas in a British one Jack Hawkins would emerge from a collapsed and flaming field hospital and murmur, "Gerry's a little restless tonight; bit of a rum go, wot?" If, as I have done, you come back to Kurt Vonnegut after once thinking you had outgrown him, that is what you appreciate—a comic tapinosis that makes Norman Mailer appear to be crying wolf.

■ I would like to write a book, let us say a novel, an historical novel, in which once in a while a page is an actual mirror. If the reader has been deluded into thinking that the book "mirrors reality" or "holds the mirror up to history," the appearance of her own reading face might serve to shock her out of that error. Imagine a mirror held up to history. It would show you history with everything happening backward. An interesting beginning of a premise, but overly limited because too passive. So no, no; any reader can hold a mirror up to a mirror held up by any writer. She will get the backward backward, get nothing more interesting than *Riel: a Documentary Poem*, or *Riel: a Documentary Drama*. But what would you do if you turned to a page, and it was a mirror? The image of your backward personal self as text. You would be compelled to relate it to the previous page and the following page.

■ I am still interested in the idea of reading as *décriture.* That is to say, the writer laid down those sentences, those lines, and now the reader picks them up from their surface. But then, go back one step. If writing is signifier, it destroys the world by turning it into strips of signified. I think of my photographer Minjus, in my western, killing off cowboys and Indians with his camera. Now, if both things are true, if writing strip-mines the referential world, and reading undoes writing, then there is at least the possibility, if we do not have some attendant instability, that reading will be a reconstituting of the world, undoing of the undoer. If writing can be deconstruction, let us say, and all reading is by nature deconstruction of the text, then reading is reconstruction, or perhaps at least renovation. In *Badlands* the photographer Sinnott remakes a gone world, whereas in the Badlands he fingered it away.

■ There is one kind of attention to sound in verse (let us say in writing poetry), and another in fiction. They resemble each other, and borrow from each other, but they are different from each other. In verse you are working on an elaborate system that begins with a certain resemblance among phonemes—prior to signification. In fiction you are dealing with sentences, whether they sound "right." When, for example, you are writing fiction, you might tell yourself to write each sentence so that it would sound good as the last sentence in the story, or in the chapter. The poet relies on his good ear. Without it he cannot write verse worth beginning to read. The short story writer is "listening" with his whole mind, and a good part of his body. Storytellers said "Once upon a time" to put listeners into hypnotic alpha-rhythms, and "they lived happily ever after" to ease them out. That's all those phrases mean.

■ One morning I walked along Inglis Street in Halifax with Ted Blodgett, the poet. We saw a sign in a shop window: "Words." Then next door we saw a pizza oven with this word on it: "Blodgett." In moments such as that, literate people start to look for meaning. Or they pretend to, and often that pretense is made in fiction or poetry or conversation. Actually Blodgett and I knew that there was no meaning in the coincidence on Inglis Street. In fact, the lack of meaning is what made the event delightful. There is a lesson for the reader of contemporary poetry in this. A poem such as Robert Kroetsch's "Sketches of a Lemon" is delightful because the connections between parts of the poem are accidental, and devoid of systematic meaning trails. The walk along Inglis Street is metonymic. It is also highly readerly. Its meaningless conjunction of words has stayed with me, as Kroetsch's poem has, while other walks in Halifax, and other poems about fruit have faded.

■ Some poets, such as Valéry, say that the importuned gods or muses supply us with a first line, and that we must then call on our poetic skill to supply as good a one as possible to resemble it. The poem is then the result of a collaboration, and keeps adding up to what it will be—a padded inspiration. In a poem called "Flowering Death," John Ashbery wrote, "We must first trick the idea/Into being, then dismantle it." Yes, there is a type of chic cynicism there, but also a modesty that becomes the serious poet. The metaphysical poet knows that his own mortality limits his poem to physical procedures. When Ashbery speaks of tricking the idea into being, he says that poets do not write to lyricize the ideas they already possess, and that their skill is musical or witty, in other words seductive or charming. But only the dismantling of the idea can make the poem or the idea live. Jefferson, for that reason, called for a revolution in every generation.

■ In an interview in *Conjunctions* 9, Edmond Jabès said, "I deeply believe that each writer carries a book in him that he will never do. All the books he writes try to approach it." Of course if he could write it, it would be *the* book; and writing, at least for him, would be at an end. I used to think that the poet strives for the perfect poem, knowing that the conditions that make him a poet also ensure that he will fail at perfection. Roland Barthes said that the permanent occupation for the writer is his cleaning up the little jobs on his desk so that he can get to work on the important book he has always had in mind. "We cannot express ourselves in a total manner," says Jabès, "only by small steps." This is what bpNichol shows you when he makes Book 8 of the *Martyrology* serve as part of Book 7. This is the meaning of a life-poem, that each moment is a reading in all directions, that you cannot outlive the closure.

■ The following remarks are a reply to Hugh Hood, but not only. Maybe it is because I was not included in the Central Canada tradition that I responded to Lawren Harris but not to the other fellows in the Group of Seven. I know that other British Columbia youngsters did too. The landscapes of the other six were trying to show how one felt about what the land looked like with no people in it amid the wind blowing. In Ontario with all its bricks, what the wild landscape looked like was very important. In Lawren Harris's paintings we knew we were not looking at what the land looked like—we were looking at what painting looked like if one did it without interruption of sentimental attachment. We had land, and landscape. Now we had painting. In Central Canada there was tradition and therefore an argument. We who grew up in British Columbia never heard it. We made art from bone.

■ We human beings have always dreamt, presumably, and we have always had some kind of explanation for our dreams. But since the invention and popularization of the motion picture, as it is called in Hollywood, we must conceive of our dreams in a way that no nineteenth century dreamer did. We must be a different kind of spectator—at least in the recounting of our dreams. Yet from the beginning the movie makers have been conscious of the dream analog. Now consider fiction. Most fiction *about* movies has been critical realism. Most dreams in fiction provide a way of softening the realistic procedure. Personally, I think that dreams are our mechanism for discarding subjects we dont need to think about any further. That is why I do not care for most of the business of dreams in fiction. They are a handy modern *deus ex machina.* We should tell people our dreams, sure, but I wouldnt make literature depend on them.

■ In my third published book of fiction, *Fiddler's Night,* I tried to find and show whatever it was that had always married realism and the openly manipulated text in my mind. Growing up when I did and where I did, I had to hunger for the sure hand of the realist text. Too young to take place in the time's central history, the second World War and the Cold War, and growing up in a town no one had ever heard of, I had to identify with Farrell's Danny O'Neill and Robbins's Danny Fisher. But growing up the town smart-ass, I was certainly not going to disappear behind the mirrors and windows of the realist's conventions. This duality is the reason why John Dos Passos was a wonderful discovery. Not really a discovery—a teacher suggested him to me. In *Fiddler's Night* the young people should have been as persuasive as those in *U.S.A.,* and the formal fiddling as irritating.

■ In the early sixties I found this passage somewhere, and assigned it to the Stupid Statements Department: "Poetry is a manoeuvering of ideas, a spectacular pleasure, achievement and mastery of intractable material, not less than an attempt to move the world, to order the chaos of man insofar as one is able. Love, harmony, order, poise, precision, new worlds." Richard Eberhart. In the late eighties, or whenever it is now, there are probably still people, even poets, who think in such terms. I cannot shake the notion that there are essentially two views of poetry. Theirs wants to manoeuver ideas, to show mastery over material, to order chaos. Ours looks after music to shape ideas, offers ourselves as servants rather than masters, and sees no chaos but a multiplicity in order. Eberhart's statement, not an unusual one, sounds in its exhuberance, very "male," like a businessman's, a developer's excitement about his potential world. We others? We sound like girlish priests, I suppose, like insect collectors, roadside talkers.

■ Robert Kroetsch is doubly carnivalistic: as soon as he heard about Bakhtin's carnivalization of the text or whatever it was, he wrote carnivals into the texts of his novels *Gone Indian* and *Badlands.* A snow carnival and a prohibition carnival—very Canadian paradoxes. Thank goodness for that bloody Kroetsch! Does this disresemble measured Ontario criticism? Piss on that! Here is a hint for the measured Ontario critics: the reason that *Badlands* starts with the sentence "I am Anna Dawe" is that *Surfacing* has an unnamed narrator. She has no name, but she has a narrating voice you cannot escape, as opposed by the dubious uncentered narrator in *Badlands. Badlands* is a carnivalization of *Surfacing.* It is the western version of the daughter's search for the drowned father.

■ The literary text has no continuous or reproductive relationship with any people, places or events in the phenomenal world. *The Invention of the World* is not in the business of mirroring Nanaimo or Brother Twelve or a Vancouver Island wedding. Neither does Jack Hodgins know all about Island mentality; nor is he a master of the English language. Every literary text is a product of various information that comes together from innumerable sources. Every author is a practitioner of knowledge and technique assembled from the output of immeasurable teachings. That is why authors have always said that they do not fully understand their own works. That is why critical readers, including the author, avail themselves of little if they seek the meanings of the author's narratemes. Rather they should piece out the ways by which he *produces* meanings. How the hell did Jack do that, a jealous author enquires of another's coup.

■ Why is it that English novels are not foreign literature but English movies are foreign films? It may be related to the fact that when you read a book, narration is made by exercising the option of turning the page, every time. But also consider this. If you are reading a novel, say J.G. Ballard's *The Concrete Island,* you have to work to supply the details of setting because the writer can only mention them, a few of them, while you can be privy to any character's thoughts, who is thinking. In a movie you can receive only (perhaps misrepresented) spoken hints of thoughts, while the camera gobbles and disgorges all the chosen minima of the physical surround. If the British author mentions a taxi we might form only an impression of the discomfort in the last one we took. In a British movie it is that strange old black high-roofed esotericism.

■ Here is the trouble with confessional poetry: the confessional poet replaces poetry's past with his own. This applies not only to the confessional poet but to any poet who is intent on expressing himself. It applies to those poets the reviewers in Toronto pick up on so easily—the poets who write lyrical anecdotes in loose unrimed lines. The ones who remind you of the immigrant experience, or the rape experience or the homestead experience. Really good poems, such as *Steveston,* do not do that, though immigrants and sexists may be mentioned during the course of the poetic event. A poem such as that, with its devotion to the words, is speaking for poetry, not for the poet. The parts of the poem are not anecdotes referring to the author's life, but something new in the reader's life. Poetry is far more potent than any poet, and there is no benefit in trying to forget that.

■ When you are trying to pull the wool over the eyes of your parent or your spouse, that person will often refer to your invention as a "likely story." She means that she does not think that she believes it. Here "likely" means "unlikely." What could be more attractive than that to a person who writes fiction? In writing fiction one always hopes for disbelief and belief at the same time. Neither would be any good or use without the other. Think about that. If *The Disinherited* were just an account of the fortunes and misfortunes of an actual rural Ontario family, who could bother to care? If it were totally invention, with no possibility of correspondence with real lives in this century, who would indulge it? It is a likely story, we say to its author, praising his literary skills while agreeing with his observations. "A likely story," your mother says, letting you know that she is going to punish you while rewarding your effort. My next novel should be subtitled "A likely story."

■ Let me not to the marriage of true minds admit Empedocles, I used to say, beginning at least to know what I meant by the *mot*. Well, we can see what the admission of Empedocles implies for fiction and poetry. Speaking of marriage, as he always was doing, he said that love and strife kept things in balance. Remember an even earlier Greek who said that strong opposition is true union. The Greeks (and their subsequent devotees), even when they spoke of discord, saw it as a part, and a necessary part, of concord. So the aestheticians till recent times prized unity as an outcome, even while promoting conflict as a step on the way. Kenneth Burke said that form consisted in setting up the reader's expectations, delaying for a while, and then satisfying them. So comedy. So, too, tragedy. Now we do not write tragedy, and we do not wind up our comedies with a wedding. We write things like the unsatisfying and terrific *The Beetle Leg*.

■ "When works of art are undergoing change," wrote Viktor Shklovsky, "interest shifts to the connective tissue." William Carlos Williams in his time told us that measure was a matter of measuring between things. Philippe Sollers said, "You cannot explain people by events but only by what, in them, resists events." And Robert Scholes said that realism's types are dedicated to the visible world while allegory's are committed to the invisible. These four men are telling us similar things, or four things about a single subject. I am presented a choice. Do I want the solace and security of a good solid representation, or conclusion, the satisfaction of aroused expectations? That is, do I want the denouement of *Duddy Kravitz*? Yes, I do, I must admit. Part of me does. The part that remembers lighting a cigarette while standing on the sidewalk after a movie. Or do I want the freefall, the attenuated explosion of Nicole Brossard's prose? I want that, too. I cant stand it, but that is what I feel a writer must enter, perhaps to pass through.

■ I believe that it is pretty well known that I like baseball, that I even write about baseball when one might expect me to be writing about other things. I often tell people that I like baseball but I dont like football and hockey, games they did not play in my home town, because they are unsubtle parodies of aggressive masculinity. But I have to say this. Some writers are like skiers, hoping to move well over the slippery terrain and not run into anything, and that's good. Some writers are like basketball players or boxers, hoping to hit the target right on, whether it is moving or not, and that is okay. Right now, or these days, I am writing like a running back, what they used to call a halfback rather than a fullback, gliding off tacklers and aspiring to make a few yards with each carry. If I am an artist, I am an escape artist, running crookedly, straight as I can.

■ I have noticed, listening to lectures or reading essays or talking with people after I have done a reading, that a lot of people who say that they are looking for meaning are really more interested in the *meant.* Even with floating signifiers and sliding signifieds, it is not enough that something is being said. People want to know what the speaker or writer means by what he says. The meant: it apparently sits there before the meaning begins and after the meaning has been done. It is a little like de Saussure's diagram, concept in both heads involved in speaking of a sentence. As I said to the novelist-poet, why do we need to investigate origins; we're here, arent we? In a poem by Robert Frost all the meaning is done to get to the meant at the end. In the *Martyrology* the meaning never stops being a verb. To me it means more than it means anything.

■ In Toronto, as in the eastern United States, people are programmed to think of Nature (the wild, the forest especially) as being "north" of them. The trees in Northern Ontario (it is western Ontario, but that name is saved for southern Ontario) are pretty small. They stack them sideways on their logging trucks. But they are still the forest "up there" in the North. A Westerner does not (yet) think that way. He sees the forest by looking out his kitchen door. As far as the Toronto imagination is concerned then, the Westerner lives in "a northern land." That is why, in the writing of Toronto people, we Westerners are often treated thematically. If a British Columbia poet arrives in town, the Toronto critic-teacher would like him to be wearing a logger's ("lumberjack's," they would say) shirt. If he writes *The Holy Forest,* they make sure that they dont know who he is.

■ In some intercontinental travelling I have been doing for literary purposes in recent years, I have come more to understand why I do not rest easy in "the Canadian tradition" espoused by some university literature teachers in Ontario and English-speaking Quebec. Of course I have always understood that. But now I have another angle on it. I think that cross-cultural similarities—sex, class, profession, whether one is a sports fan, etc.—outpace in-cultural groupings. The implications for writing, and especially for criticism and theory, are many and enspiriting. You will notice that our critics are quicker to pick up the European critics than they are the new Canadian poetry. I find it easier to make my notions known to my confreres and sisters in New Zealand and Italy than to Canadian literary journalists. I know an Australian who knows more about *Alibi* than any reviewer in my own country. I will remind myself to write local histories for foreigners.

■ All my life I have been reading, reading as much as I can, buying books faster than I can read them, hoping at first that I could read everything, later knowing that I will perish with books I paid good money for lying unread on the shelves and floor. And what for? You cant take it with you. Well, yes you can. When you die you take everything you have read into the grave with you. So with writing. Even if my books remain in print when and if I am gone, and if they are read by men and women then, those people are going to take my books nowhere but to the grave. If people read my books two thousand years from now, if there are any people or books two thousand years from now, unless there is medical immortality those books will go with the kaput humanoids whose atoms will likely be sprayed into the psychosphere. So why do we do it, why write books? So *we* can read them, of course, before it is too late.

■ The idea of Eastern Canada was keenly exotic to me when I was a schoolboy. Of course at that time Eastern Canada was anything from Regina on back. It was exotic as schoolbooks, those schoolbooks that we could see were addressed to some hardly imaginable children back east, where grandparents seemingly lived on farms with barns and silos and several radio stations. In school we covered our textbooks with Bank of Montreal brown paper, which we tried to learn to cut and fold and lick and stick. It was awful to have loose corners all year. There was no Bank of Montreal in our town. It was another exotic and eastern thing, like Frontenac. Usually the books under the covers (which I tried to wear off "accidentally" over the weeks) were old, used. I just loved the rare crisp new textbooks, any subject. I longed to write in them, to underline something, to do my name neatly, the way I had decided my signature would look, to put my western pen-nib to that confident print.

■ One loves only form, said Olson, and form comes into being when the thing is born. I think that there can be no doubt about that, no getting around it. Beauty creates love, and beauty makes one want art. But some dolts, while extolling an emotional outburst about love, will denigrate the intellect as if it were a tight collar. What a pity. Great beauty reveals itself the more fully as it moves the mind. And mind is shared; the experience of the mind is shared experience. John Keats, whose writing can be found to influence Olson, and earlier Williams, wrote some great earthly beauty, and did not want to know too much about it. But ragged Shelley is, to my mind, the greater poet, because the heaven he was trying to glimpse could be approached only in thought, the achieved shaping of thought, only in the forms granted to and by the human mind in imagination.

■ Quite frequently I am bothered by the old question of "the author's intention." As an author I am aware that my intention is important to me, something I dont like to see mistaken. But I am also aware that I court conditions, especially in poetry, under which my intentions will be thwarted, whereby my will will be subverted. I am a west coast member of Oulipo. Here is one thing I know about observing and perhaps understanding: intentions are easier to read than are reasons. What is she trying to do is an easier question than why is she doing that. In school the teacher or the textbook asked what is (or was) the author's intention and how successful was he in achieving his purpose? Somewhat later it became unsophisticated or even crude to ask that question. The teachers who had heard of the criticism of the New Critics said it was an insult to notice the author at all. Now that we have the author back, even if he is dead, we can and will ask, for example, what is he trying to do by calling them *The Maximus Poems* rather than the Olson poems.

■ Think of the U.S.A. in 1961, a hundred years after the beginning of the big American war about race and region, not a case of one becoming two, but many trying to figure out how, with the usual American violence, to become one. One hundred years later they have Jack Kennedy and Jack Kerouac. *On The Road* somewhere in the New Frontier. The president had what was then thought to be a lot of hair, and was rumoured to have smoked dope, being a kind of rich hipster on the square side. But more than that, he was a Catholic. That was a big deal in 1961. If the president of the U.S.A. was going to lean that far away from the idea of Calvin Coolidge, then the messy-hair, dope-tasting Quebec Catholic American king of the Beats would have to take over the literary oval office. But you remember who was the poet at Kennedy's inauguration. Yes, Robert Frost. The Open Road is still free from the friendly squares.

■ Some writers are very good with titles. Audrey Thomas and Michael Ondaatje consider their titles very carefully. Audrey stole one from me, but I dont mind. You will notice that most of these errata mention a title. They are interesting things, titles. I generally have lots left over. The working title for my novel *Burning Water* was *The Dead Sailors.* Some magazine publications of excerpts in progress mentioned that name. The publisher's audience-understanding machine said that readers are not attracted to titles with dead in them. But detective-book readers are, I said. Besides, most of the famous literary stories about sailors are about dead sailors: Coleridge, Shakespeare, Melville, I said. You'll have to come up with a new title, the publisher said. My previous publisher had told me I'd have to come up with a different ending. That would have been worse. But how to rename a book? If it were a racehorse, I would call it G. Delsing, son of Misery, out of Perfection.

■ What would I rename *The Dead Sailors*? I thought of *The King's Albatross* and *The Mariner's Trance* and *The Dash of Oars* and *The Devil Knows How to Row* and *Man and Bird and Beast* and *The North West Passion* and *Floating Island* and *Soundings at the Edge* and *Pacific Sounds* and *Kings and Sailors* (this is a little enjoyable, isnt it?) and *Islands* and *Sails* and *HMS Prospero* and *Empire Fancy* and *Captain Caliban* and *Sailing Into Vision* and *The Imaginary Sailors* (yes, I know all these are not quite it) and *His Majesty's Mariner* and *Where Lies the Land* and *A Painted Ocean* and *Fog and Fire* and *Arrows of Desire* and *The Deep Nook* and *The King my Father's Wrack* and *Something Rich and Strange* and *No Mortal Business* and *The Great Globe Itself* and *The Sixth Hour* and *Drown my Book* and *Where the Bee Sucks* and *Bring Forth a Wonder* and *A Vision of the Island* and *Second Life, Second Father* and *Particular Accidents* and *Auspicious Gales*.

■ I have always been aware of a difference between the Vancouver avant-garde and the Toronto avant-garde. The activities of the Toronto avant-garde are carried on with consciousness of the goings-on in fashion. If their art is documented, the Vancouver avant-gardistes do the documentation as another of their alienated but community-oriented events. Documentation in Toronto is always reaching toward the public, the official: the people involved want to say look what we interesting people are doing, dont you wish we were at your parties? I dont know whether this is connected, but in the sixties living in Vancouver was living long days of marijuana, LSD, peyote and mushrooms. If you visited Toronto you would notice people around you taking speed or sniffing something. Well, Toronto's official art believes itself to be Canada's official art. Maybe the avant-garde people feel the write-man's (video-woman's) burden.

■ For years I went around saying that poetry is a spoken art, and that fiction should, when possible, be written as poetry is, the writer keeping in mind the notion that he is transcribing voice for his prose. I still like to hear the speaker inside my cranium while I'm putting ink, somehow, to paper. But now I think, perhaps, the way a playwright thinks, marking down something that will only later be spoken. Now I think that reading came first, as our intelligent forebears would read the sky, the earth and the sea for the information they needed to find there. In Westerns it is called "reading sign." The tracker, with an occluded wisdom, can read something that is invisible to the rest of us. After some time came writing, as some of our forebears took advantage of reading, and made messages, a few rocks placed in a pattern, say, to become the information to be found. Finally, third, came speech, an alternative to writing. Some scientists in Berkeley proposed that speech was a genetic accident that became a Darwinian advantage. Samuel Beckett said that words are a form of complacency.

■ I have always had, when I am reading a book, a double feeling. Part of me is noticing the pleasure of the moment, of the page; and the other part of me is anticipating getting the reading done, the book finished. The less the moment's enjoyment, the more the anticipation of the end, of course. But even while reading a thoroughly loveable book, as for example *Alibi,* there is that expectation of the moment when its back cover will go smack onto the gathered pages. Some voice from within, edging past the puritan substance, might ask: why leap to read a book if you aim at no longer reading it? Isnt that something akin to the pleasure of ceasing to bang one's forehead against the wall? No, say I, because despite what one's rough friends said, reading is not an alternative to living, but one of its finer manifestations. And there are so many more books, already in one's rooms, or within walking distance.

■ I think that the fiction writer begins to depart from realism when she replaces the referent with the signified. It was a fine romance, the affair between the reference and the designated world. The sign was part of a design. What was Anne? She was *Anne of Green Gables.* She did not have green gables on her the way *The House of the Seven Gables* had seven gables on it. If you go to Green Gables today they will show you the golf course and Anne's room upstairs in the clubhouse. You can just picture Anne there, and the other girl. The main purpose of the referent is to be unmistakable. But the sign now: think of all the times when the sign has to be mistakable. The coach flashes the sign to the hitter. Only the semi-mystical Indian scout can read three-day-old outlaw sign. The deaf can sign and so can the executive, and we ordinary literary types find both illegible.

■ One gets attracted to the phenomenologists as one did to the skeptics, especially liking the ones whose names begin with the firm letter H: Hume, Husserl, Heidegger, because clear trustworthy demon-stration is so much more exciting than a trickle-down from abstraction. What are you looking at, they will ask you in college, and you will say that you can supply only the name of something you think you are looking at. But the rigor always leads to transcendentalism, as it did even for systematic overly German Husserl. The *epochē*, meant to reduce, opens wide to the meta-physical multiverse. That's what my postcard poem was about:

> I went to the blackberries
> on the vine.
>
> They were blackberries
> on the vine.
>
> They were
> blackberries.
>
> Black
> berries.

■ In a 1972 interview with Ludovic Janvier, Claude Simon said, "Proust's *Recherché* didnt lead him to regain time, but to produce a written object which has its own temporality." Let us put it in scholarly terms, too. There is really no such thing as research. There is only search, more search, keep on searching. Really, even Proust knew that, and why not? The painters around him had shown the way, as painters always do. You do not need a reference to nature to create non-nature, or art. The reader does not need to go back and check. The reader can check right here, right now, inside the text. The Kilgore Trout in the first chapter was not real, was not Theodore Sturgeon. He was a whole other kettle of fish. The Kilgore Trout in the last chapter may be checked against the one in the first chapter, and back to another book. But none of that time was ever *perdu*.

■ One does not want to create and write a new language; rather one wants to work out a new relationship with language. One wants to speak inside the dominant discourse, but if one is thinking at all, one is perforce bilingual. Inside the dominant discourse one is tradition, working tradition. Damn it, I will say it this way. Or damn it, why did no one see this beauty before now? The tradition is formed from an accretion of the avant-garde. The people who proclaim their congratulated adherence to "traditional forms" are generally the (unwitting?) enemies of the tradition. Like science, the avant-garde hopes to see its current manifestations cast aside or at least modified in the future. Coming along one hundred years later and referring to them as "traditional forms" is to betray the avant-garde and the tradition.

■ [Aug. 1964, Mexico] Ezra Pound's translations, as much as his poems, work to make ground for subsequent artists to work upon (as do his essays—a plan, a project). Their purpose is not only to make a stab at the past, but to provide for the community of poets (of all time). So for me, who desires to work in that community; my concern need not be to test or carp about the fidelity of the translations, *Umbra* and the rest. Either I learn something from the resulting poems, or I dont. Or at least I can find the poems enjoyable; I can be kept to the page, the Poundian page now. Hugh Kenner says: "The Poundian homage consists in taking an earlier poet as guide to secret places of the imagination." In twenty-five years I will agree with that language. But what if the present were the world's last night? Read Arnault Daniel, by Ezra Pound.

■ [Aug. 1964, Mexico] To say something about Ezra Pound's translations is like trying to say something adequate about Notre Dame Cathedral or the *Bellas Artes.* Pound is apart (and consequently beyond), one of the few titans who stand astride all the rest of the work being done in this age. It may someday be seen to be Pound's greatest achievement that he has brought a thousand pages of verse tradition to us, so that we be not restricted by the insular interests of the English faculty and the market-conscious anthologers. As an example of what I mean: I was asked recently by a lady professor from England, now teaching in Canada: "Do you mean seriously to say that Pound is anywhere near as good as Auden?" You see, it can and does happen. In twenty-five years it may still be happening if there are still Englishmen.

■ If poetry were *about* life there would be no reason to study it or love it. But as it is a living world itself, one studies it for the same reasons that one goes into any world. Or similar reasons, anyway. Soul stomps his foot; spirit lifts her wings. These are not messages but the news themselves. Ezra Pound once said to his daughter Mary: "I dont want you to understand; I want you to learn the damn thing!" One knows in one's youth that *The Cantos* that baffle and unnerve one are a great poem to be read for a lifetime. [<L *studere,* to be zealous or eager]. To strike like a friend. If poetry were simply *about* life it would be no more loveable than sociology. People who think that words are tools also think that poetry is about life. They usually have no time for sports. They think that philosophy is wasted time. Children: listen to Phaedrus.

■ One of my favourite endings to a book is the last ten pages of *Alibi.* Dorf's journal seems to be starting something new, and then the book is gone. So is hope of resolution, comfort, redemption, rest. Solace. Most books have opened up with the first promise of closure. A novel is much like the history of an illness. Near the beginning we see the breaking of calm, the disruption of order, the discomfort of the disease. The fever runs its course for a few hundred pages. At the end the little history is complete, the patient probably discharged. The result is sometimes a complete cure; more often there is a kind of accommodation of some wound (see Ernest Hemingway or Margaret Laurence), and a hint of harmony and art's re-creation of the aging soul. What of a writer who delays closure? Maybe he should see a doctor. Maybe he *is* the doctor.